LUCY D

Little
Animal Ark™

The Lucky Lamb

Hodder
Children's
Books

A division of Hachette Children's Books

To Lynne Bradbury, dear friend, with love

Special thanks to Narinder Dhami

Little Animal Ark is a trademark of Working Partners Limited
Text copyright © 2002 Working Partners Limited
Created by Working Partners Limited, London, W6 0QT
Illustrations copyright © 2002 Andy Ellis

First published in Great Britain in 2002 by Hodder Children's Books

This edition published in 2007

The rights of Lucy Daniels and Andy Ellis to be identified as the author
and illustrator of this work respectively have been asserted by them in
accordance with the Copyright, Designs and Patents Act 1988.

7

A Catalogue record for this book is available from the
British Library

ISBN-13: 978 0 340 93256 8

Printed and bound in Great Britain by
Clays Ltd, St Ives plc

The paper and board used in this paperback by Hodder Children's
Books are natural recyclable products made from wood grown in
sustainable forests. The manufacturing processes conform to the
environmental regulations of the country of origin.

Hodder Children's Books
A division of Hachette Children's Books
338 Euston Road, London NW1 3BH
An Hachette UK Company
www.hachette.co.uk

Chapter One

"Dad, is it time for my surprise now?" Mandy Hope asked eagerly. She finished her apple pie and custard, and put down her spoon. "I've been waiting for ages!"

Mr Hope laughed. "Just let me finish my pudding, Mandy!" he said.

"Mandy's going to burst if she doesn't find out what the surprise is soon," Mrs Hope said with a smile.

"I'm so full, I think I *might* burst!" Mandy joked, patting her tummy. "That was a lovely lunch. Thanks, Gran."

Mandy and her mum and dad were having Sunday lunch with Gran and Grandad Hope. On the way to Lilac Cottage, Mr Hope had told Mandy that he had a surprise for her. She couldn't wait to find out what it was. All she knew was that they would have to go in the Land-rover.

Mandy hoped it was something to do with animals. Mandy *loved* animals! Her mum and dad were vets at Animal Ark, and Mandy wanted to be a vet too one day.

"Anyone for seconds?" her gran asked. She picked up the jug of custard.

"Not for me, thanks," Mr Hope said. "I'd better not keep Mandy waiting any longer!"

"Don't worry," said Mandy's grandad. "I'll finish up the rest of the apple pie!"

Mandy dashed into the hall to get her coat. She wondered where her dad was taking her.

"I'm ready, Dad," she said, rushing back into the living-room. Just then, she spotted her gran's knitting bag and remembered something important. "I've got something to ask Gran," she said.

"What's that?" Gran smiled.

"We're doing a project at school," Mandy said. "And tomorrow we're looking at all the things we can do with wool."

"That sounds interesting," said

Mr Hope, putting on his jacket.

"So we've all got to take something woolly to school," Mandy went on. "Could you lend me a ball of wool from your knitting bag, Gran?"

"Of course," said Mandy's gran.

The knitting bag was full of different colours. Mandy chose a big ball of thick yellow wool.

Her gran seemed to have rather a lot of it. "Can I have this one, Gran?" she asked.

"That's the wool I'm using to knit your dad a jumper," said Grandma Hope. "Make sure you bring it back. Or your dad will have a jumper with only one sleeve!"

"That sounds a bit chilly," Mr Hope said with a grin.

"And you can borrow the knitting pattern as well," Grandma Hope added. "It might be interesting to see how the wool will be turned into a jumper."

"Thanks, Gran," Mandy beamed. She gave the ball and

the pattern to her mum.

Mrs Hope put them in her
bag to take home.

"Are we going now, Dad?"
Mandy asked.

"We're going *right* now," Mr
Hope laughed.

At last Mandy was going to
find out what her surprise was.
She couldn't wait!

Chapter Two

"Dad, isn't this the way to
Deepdale Farm?" Mandy asked,
as the Land-rover bumped along
a narrow track.

"It might be," said Mr Hope.

"Oh, Dad!" Mandy laughed.
"I *know* it is. Liam White lives
there. He's in the Reception class
at school."

Mandy was in Class 3
at Welford Primary School.

She knew Liam, but not very well. Why was her dad taking her to Deepdale Farm? "Is one of the farm animals ill, Dad?" she asked.

"Not as far as I know," said Mr Hope. He pulled into the farmyard and parked the Land-rover. The farmhouse door opened, and Liam and his mum came out.

"Hi, Mandy," Liam called, waving at her. "I've been waiting for you."

Mandy waved back. She couldn't help staring at Liam. He was wearing the most amazing jumper that Mandy had ever seen! It was bright red and it had a picture of a white, woolly lamb on the front.

Liam grinned.

"Do you like my jumper,
Mandy?" he asked. "Look at the
back!" He turned round.

Mandy burst out laughing.
On the back of the jumper was
the *back* of the woolly lamb.
There was even a little woolly
tail hanging down, which swung
about
when
Liam
moved.
"It's
great,
Liam!"
she said.

"Liam's granny made it for him," Mrs White told Mandy with a smile. "And if Liam had his way, he'd never take it off!"

"It's my best jumper," Liam agreed.

Mr Hope smiled. "Liam's jumper should give you a clue about why we're here, Mandy," he said.

Mandy felt puzzled for a minute. But then her face lit up. "Dad!" she said. "Are we here to see some lambs?"

Her dad nodded. "The very *first* newborn lamb of the season," he said. "How about that?"

"Oh!" Mandy gasped. This *had* been a surprise worth waiting for!

"The lamb is in the barn with his mum," Liam said. He slipped his hand into Mandy's. "And guess what? My dad said I could choose his name," he told her proudly.

"What have you called him?" Mandy asked, as they walked across the farmyard.

"I'll tell you when you've seen him," Liam promised. He led Mandy and Mr Hope into the barn.

A sheep lay on a pile of straw with a tiny white lamb pressed close to her side. Mr White was kneeling beside them.

"Oh!" Mandy breathed. She looked closely at the little lamb. His coat was tightly-curled and snowy-white. He had big, dark eyes and a little snub nose. "He's *lovely*!" she said.

The lamb lifted his head when he heard the visitors. His legs were a bit wobbly, but he struggled to his feet and stared at them. *"Maaaa!"* he bleated loudly.

Liam tugged at Mandy's hand. "I called him Woolly," he said. "Do you think that's a good name?"

Mandy smiled. "It's a *brilliant* name," she answered. She bent down and stroked Woolly's white head. Then she saw that Mr White was looking worried.

"I'm glad you're here, Adam," Mr White said to Mandy's dad. "I think there's something wrong with Woolly's mum."

Mandy looked at the sheep.
She was lying very still.

Mr Hope checked the sheep over. "She needs to rest," he said with a frown. "Woolly's mum is too weak to look after him. He'll need stay indoors until his mum is stronger."

Mr White carefully picked up the lamb. Woolly bleated loudly. His tiny black hooves scrabbled against Mr White's jacket.

"Poor Woolly," Mandy said sadly. "He wants to stay with his mum."

Mr White carried Woolly over to the farmhouse. Mandy and Liam went with him, while Mr Hope stayed with Woolly's mum.

"I'd better go back to the barn," Mr White said, as he put Woolly down in the kitchen.

"Don't worry, Dad," Liam said. "We'll look after Woolly."

Mrs White went off to get some blankets to make a bed for the lamb.

Woolly was very interested in everything in the kitchen. He ran under the table and sniffed the chairs.

He jumped about on the rug in front of the fire, kicking up his little hooves.

Then he trotted over to the washing-machine. A basket of washing was next to it, waiting to be put in. Woolly leaned into the basket to take a look. When he pulled his head out again, he had a pillowcase stuck on it!

"Maaaa!" he bleated, trying to shake the pillowcase off.

"Oh, poor Woolly!" Mandy said, grinning.

Mandy and Liam rushed over and pulled the pillowcase off the lamb's head.

Woolly shook his head and looked much happier.

"I've found this box and some blankets," said Mrs White, coming back into the kitchen. "Liam, you and Mandy can make a bed for Woolly."

So Mandy and Liam tucked the blankets neatly into the box, and made a lovely nest for the little lamb.

Woolly seemed to like his new bed a lot. He climbed in and snuggled down cosily.

"Don't worry, Woolly," Mandy whispered, stroking the lamb's soft coat. "Your mum will be better soon. Then you can be together again."

Chapter Three

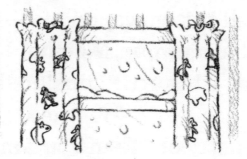

"Oh, *look* at the snow!" Mandy gasped, as she pulled back her bedroom curtains.

It was the next morning. It had snowed all night. The village and the fields were covered with a thick, white blanket.

Mrs Hope popped her head round the door while Mandy was getting dressed. "Put a jumper over your school sweatshirt, Mandy," she said. "It's really cold today."

"OK, Mum," Mandy said. She opened her drawer and took out a cosy blue jumper. Her gran had knitted it for her. "I don't really

 need Gran's ball of wool now," she joked, pulling the jumper over her head. "I've got my nice thick jumper for our wool lesson!"

Her mum laughed. "I should think most of your friends will be taking a woolly jumper to school today," she said.

"I'll *still* take Gran's wool," Mandy decided. "It'll be really boring if everyone just brings a jumper!"

As Mandy followed her mum downstairs, she wondered how Woolly and his mum were. She would be able to ask Liam when she got to school.

After breakfast, Mrs Hope walked to school with Mandy.

As she walked through the gate, Mandy spotted Liam in the

infants' playground. He was making snowballs with his friends. "Liam!" she called. "How's Woolly?"

Liam came over, shaking snow from his gloves. "Woolly's fine!" he beamed. "But he's a bit naughty. He was chasing our cat, George, round the kitchen last night!"

Mandy laughed. "What about his mum?" she asked.

"She's a bit better," Liam said. "And guess what – five more lambs were born last night!"

"That's great!" Mandy said. "Maybe I'll be able to come with Dad when he visits. Then I'd be able to see Woolly again, and all the other new lambs!" Mandy grinned at Liam. "I bet you're wearing your lamb jumper under your coat, aren't you?"

Liam's smile faded. "No, Mum wanted to wash it today," he sighed.

Just then the bell rang.

"See you later!" Mandy called.

She ran off to line up with her class in the Juniors' playground. Five more lambs! She couldn't wait to meet them.

"We have a visitor this morning, Class 3," said Mandy's teacher, Miss Rushton.

Mandy wondered who it could be.

"It's someone who knows a lot about wool," Miss Rushton went on. "One of our local farmers – Mr White."

"Great!" Mandy whispered to Peter Foster, who was sitting next to her. Liam's dad was coming to visit their class! She'd be able to ask him all about the newborn lambs.

"Now let's see what woolly things you've brought to school today," Miss Rushton said, smiling. "Peter, would you like to go first? What have you got to show us?"

Peter had brought some sheep's wool that he'd found stuck on the hedgerows.

Richard Tanner showed everyone a picture his mum had sewn, using brightly-coloured wool.

Pippa Simkins had brought some woolly socks, which looked very warm and cosy.

33

Then it was Mandy's turn. She stood at the front of the class, and showed everyone the ball of yellow wool and the knitting pattern. "My gran's making my dad a jumper out of this wool," she said. "And she told me I have to give it back, or Dad will have a jumper with only one sleeve!"

Everyone laughed. But before Mandy could say any more, the classroom door opened.

It was Mr White. But he wasn't on his own. The farmer was carrying something in his arms. A little lamb . . .

Chapter Four

"Mr White has brought a *special* visitor with him!" Miss Rushton laughed. "I think Mandy knows him already."

Mandy could hardly believe her eyes. "It's Woolly!" she told everyone excitedly.

Woolly bleated loudly, and butted his head against Mandy's hand.

"Woolly's the first lamb to be

born this season," Mr White explained.

Everyone was thrilled to see Woolly. And Woolly seemed keen to say hello to everyone!

Miss Rushton clapped her hands. "Quiet now, please," she said firmly. "You'll get a chance to play with Woolly later."

Mr White sat down on a chair at the front, so everyone could see Woolly.

"Now, Mandy," Miss Rushton said. "Tell us more about what you've brought to show us."

"This is my gran's knitting pattern," Mandy said. "It tells her how to make the jumper – OH!"

Woolly had leaned over and started nibbling the corner of Grandma Hope's pattern! Everyone gasped, then laughed.

"Woolly, stop that!" Mr White said sternly. But he was smiling too. He put Woolly down on the floor, so the lamb couldn't reach the pattern.

As Mandy watched, she dropped Grandma Hope's ball of wool. It rolled towards Woolly, and began to unwind.

The lamb looked at the yellow ball. He pulled away from Mr White's hands and bent down to sniff it. He wagged his tail. Then he kicked the ball with one of his tiny hooves!

While everyone watched, Woolly jumped backwards and forwards over his new toy. But the wool began to tangle round Woolly's legs. He tried to kick it off. And the more Woolly jumped about, the more tangled up he got!

"Oh, Woolly!" Mandy gasped. She hoped he wouldn't hurt himself. And what about her gran's wool? Mandy had promised to get it back to her safely.

Mr White tried to catch his lamb. But Woolly was having too much fun! He dashed to the other side of the classroom, leaving a trail of yellow wool behind him.

"Be careful, Woolly!" Mandy called.

Mr White finally caught Woolly and picked him up. "Don't worry, Mandy," he said. "Your gran's wool will be fine."

Mandy helped Mr White to free Woolly from the yellow wool.

Miss Rushton wound the wool up again. Soon Grandma Hope's ball of wool looked as good as new.

"Oh, Woolly!" Mandy laughed. She patted him on the head. "You must be the naughtiest lamb in the whole world!"

"They're lovely, aren't they, Dad?" Mandy said softly. They were looking at the newborn lambs in the barn. Mr Hope had come to pick up Mandy and Liam after school, on his way to Deepdale Farm. He wanted to check up on Woolly's mum again.

"Is Woolly's mum all better now, Mr Hope?" Liam asked.

"Nearly, Liam," Mr Hope said, smiling.

Mandy looked at Woolly's mum. She was standing up now. And she looked much happier. "So can Woolly come back out to the barn?" Mandy asked eagerly.

Her dad shook his head. "No, love. It's too cold at the moment," he said. "Woolly's used to being in the warm farmhouse now."

"It *is* cold, even here in the barn," Mandy said. She shivered.

"Yes, we need to warm up," said Mr White. "Come into the house and have some hot chocolate."

It was very cosy in the

farmhouse. Mrs White was in the kitchen with Woolly. He came running over to meet them.

"Hello, Woolly," Mandy said, stroking the lamb's soft ears. "I haven't got any wool for you to play with this time!"

Mr White poured some milk into a saucepan and put it on the cooker to warm up. Mandy saw that Mrs White looked a bit upset. She wondered why.

Then Mrs White turned to Liam. "I'm really sorry, Liam, but there's been a bit of an accident," she said. She held out something for Liam to see.

Mandy gasped. It was Liam's lamb jumper. But it had shrunk!

Chapter Five

"Mum!" Liam wailed. "What's happened to my lamb jumper?"

Mrs White looked even more upset. "It shrunk when I washed it," she said sadly. "The water must have been too hot."

Liam rushed over to the jumper and stared at it. He reached out and stroked the lamb. The jumper was far too small for him now.

"I'm sure Granny will knit you another one," Mrs White said, giving Liam a hug. "Come on, let's have some hot chocolate and biscuits. I've got the ones with jam in. Your favourites."

Mandy could tell that Liam was trying hard not to cry.

She felt so sorry for him that she had a lump in her throat. She could hardly drink her hot chocolate or eat her biscuits. Liam didn't touch his at all.

"*Maaaa!*" Woolly bleated.

Mandy jumped. She had almost forgotten about Woolly. He had squeezed under the table and was butting everyone's legs with his head.

"I think Woolly's feeling a bit left out," said Mr White. "It's time for his bottle. Do you and Mandy want to help me feed him, Liam?"

Liam nodded, but he still looked upset. Mandy sat down next to him on the sofa.

She couldn't think of anything to say to make him feel better.

Mr White put Woolly in between Mandy and Liam. Then he held out the bottle. At once, Woolly grabbed it and began to suck as hard as he could. He made funny slurping noises.

Mandy looked at Liam. He was smiling as he watched Woolly feeding noisily. Woolly had made Liam forget how sad he was about his lamb jumper.

"It's a shame Woolly can't be with his mum," Liam said, stroking the lamb's back. "It could be ages before the weather gets warmer."

Suddenly, an idea popped into Mandy's head. "Oh!" she gasped. "I think I know how we can keep Woolly warm enough!"

Everyone stared at her. "How?" Liam asked.

Mandy grinned at him. "What Woolly needs is *another* woolly jumper to put on top of his own. And I know just the one!"

Chapter Six

Liam's eyes lit up. "My lamb jumper!" he cried. "Do you think it will fit Woolly now?"

Mandy looked at Mr Hope. "What do you think, Dad?" she asked.

"I think it's a great idea," Mr Hope agreed, smiling. "But the jumper will smell very strange to Woolly's mum," he warned. "She might not like it."

"Is there anything we could do, Mr Hope?" Liam asked.

"Well, you could rub the jumper with straw from the barn," said Mr Hope.

"And also rub it on Woolly's mum's coat," said Mr White. "Then the jumper will have smells that Woolly's mum knows."

"Let's go and do it right now!" Liam said eagerly.

Woolly had finished his bottle, so Mr White lifted him on to the floor.

Mandy and Liam jumped up. Smiling, Mrs White handed them the jumper, and they ran off to the barn.

Liam got a handful of straw and rubbed it all over the jumper. Then Mandy took the jumper and rubbed it against Woolly's mum's coat. The sheep looked a bit surprised, but she stayed still.

"You're going to see your lamb really soon!" Mandy whispered.

She patted the sheep on her head.

Mandy and Liam took the jumper back to the farmhouse. It was time to dress Woolly!

The lamb didn't seem very keen at first. As Mr Hope tugged the jumper over his head, Woolly bleated loudly and tried to get away. But, at last, Woolly was dressed!

"You look so sweet, Woolly," Mandy laughed, giving the lamb a hug.

Woolly looked quite proud of his new outfit! He trotted out of the kitchen behind Liam and Mandy, happily kicking up his little hooves.

They led him over to the barn.
The wind was cold outside, but
Woolly didn't seem to notice.

Mandy hoped that Woolly's mum wouldn't mind him wearing the jumper. She held her breath and watched as Woolly trotted over to his mum with a cheerful bleat.

Woolly's mum sniffed the jumper. She looked a bit puzzled. She sniffed it again. Then Woolly cuddled up close to her, and they gently rubbed their heads together.

"I don't mind about my jumper now," Liam said with a big smile. "I'm just glad that Woolly's back with his mum."

Mandy felt very pleased that her idea had worked out so well. "Woolly's lucky to have such a special jumper," she laughed. "He is a really lucky lamb!"

Chapter One

"How many hot cross buns are you going to make for the Easter festival, Gran?" Mandy Hope asked. She munched a biscuit as she watched her gran write a shopping list.

Grandma Hope put down her pen. "About two hundred," she said. "There are always lots of people at church for the Easter service."

"Can I help you make them?"
Mandy asked. She was staying at
her gran and grandad's for the
day. Her mum and dad were both
working. They were vets at
Animal Ark. Mandy wanted to be
a vet too when she grew up.

Her gran smiled. "I was
hoping you would," she said. "We
can start baking this afternoon
after we've been shopping."

While Grandma Hope finished
the list of what they needed,
Mandy looked at the cookery book.
Next to the recipe was a picture of
a baby rabbit, sniffing a huge pile
of hot cross buns.

Mandy grinned. "Look, it's

an Easter bunny, Gran," she said. Suddenly her eyes widened. She'd just had an idea. A really *great* idea!

"Gran!" she gasped. "We should have animals at the church on Sunday. They're part of Easter. They could come to the festival too."

Grandma Hope nodded. "You know, that sounds lovely, Mandy," she said.

"We could have baby rabbits and chicks – and lambs . . ." Mandy went on.

"Lambs might be a bit of a handful," Mandy's gran said with a smile. "But I'm sure everyone would love to have rabbits and chicks in the church. Why don't we go to the vicarage and ask Reverend Hadcroft?"

"Yes, let's!" Mandy cried, jumping to her feet.

Twenty minutes later, Mandy and her gran were sitting in Reverend

Hadcroft's living room.

"I think it's an excellent idea," Reverend Hadcroft said. "Do you think you can organise it, Mandy?"

"Oh yes," Mandy said. She looked at her gran. "Laura Baker's coming to the festival with her mum and dad. She might like to bring Nibbles, her rabbit. We could call in and ask her on the way home."

"Good idea," said Grandma Hope.